召树屯

岩叠 陈贵培 刘绮 王松 翻译整理
陈兰芳 英译 [美] H. W. Lan 审校

国家出版基金项目
NATIONAL PUBLICATION FOUNDATION

"十三五"国家重点图书
中国南方民间文学典籍英译丛书
丛书主编 张立玉 丛书副主编 起国庆

ZHAO SHU TUN

出品单位：
中南民族大学南方少数民族文库翻译研究基地
云南省少数民族古籍整理出版规划办公室

WUHAN UNIVERSITY PRESS
武汉大学出版社

·汉英对照·

图书在版编目(CIP)数据

召树屯:汉英对照/岩叠等翻译整理;陈兰芳英译.—武汉:武汉大学出版社,2020.6(2022.1 重印)

中国南方民间文学典籍英译丛书/张立玉主编

“十三五”国家重点图书　2020 年度国家出版基金资助项目

ISBN 978-7-307-21453-8

Ⅰ.召…　Ⅱ.①岩…　②陈…　Ⅲ.傣族—叙事诗—中国—汉、英
Ⅳ.I222.7

中国版本图书馆 CIP 数据核字(2020)第 060710 号

责任编辑:罗晓华　　责任校对:李孟潇　　版式设计:韩闻锦

出版发行:**武汉大学出版社**　(430072　武昌　珞珈山)
(电子邮箱:cbs22@whu.edu.cn　网址:www.wdp.whu.edu.cn)

印刷:湖北恒泰印务有限公司

开本:720×1000　1/16　印张:9.25　字数:108 千字

版次:2020 年 6 月第 1 版　2022 年 1 月第 2 次印刷

ISBN 978-7-307-21453-8　定价:29.00 元

序

近年来，民族典籍英译捷报频传，硕果累累。韩家全教授等人的壮族系列经典翻译陆续出版，王宏印教授等人的系列民族典籍英译研究著作已经问世，李正栓教授等人的藏族格言诗英译著作不断在国内外出版，王维波教授等人的东北民族典籍英译著作纷纷付梓，李昌银教授等人的“云南少数民族经典作品英译文库”于2018年年底出版，其他民族典籍英译作品也在接踵而至。

近日，中南民族大学张立玉教授传来佳音：他们要出版“十三五”国家重点图书——“中国南方民间文学典籍英译丛书”。虽叫民间文学，其实基本上都是民族典籍。这一系列包括十本书，它们是《黑暗传》《哭嫁歌》《哈尼阿培聪坡坡》《彝族民间故事》《南方民间创世神话选集》《查姆》《召树屯》《娥并与桑洛》《金笛》《梅葛》。其中，好几本是云南少数民族的。只有一本是汉族典籍，即《黑暗传》。很有意思的是，这些典籍展示了不同民族的创世史诗或诸如此类的东西。

《黑暗传》以民间歌谣唱本形象地描述了盘古开天辟地结束混沌黑暗、人类起源及社会发展的历程，融合了混沌、盘古、女娲、伏羲、炎帝神农氏、黄帝轩辕氏等众多英雄人物在洪荒时代艰难创世的一系列神话传说。它被称为汉族首部创世史诗。《哈尼阿培聪坡坡》是一部完整地记载哈尼族历史沿革的长篇史诗，堪称哈尼族的“史记”，长5000余行，以现实主义手法记叙了哈尼族祖先在各个历史时期的迁徙情况，并对其迁徙各地的原因、路线、途程，各个迁居地的社会生活、生产、风习、宗教，以及与毗邻民族的关系等，均作了详细而生动的辑录，因而该作品不仅具有文学价值，而且具有重大的历史学、社会学及宗教学价值。《南方民间创世神话选集》包括一些创世神话，主要是关于世界起源和人类起源的神话。本书所列包括生活在广泛地域的民族，如门巴族、珞巴族、怒族、基诺族、普米族、拉祜族、傈僳族、毛南族、德昂族、景颇族、阿昌族、布朗族、佤族、独龙族、水族、仡佬族、布依族、仫佬族、高山族和侗族等。这些神话不仅讲述了世界的起源，也讲述了人类的始祖，以及人类对世界的改造。《梅葛》是彝族的一部长篇史诗，流传在云南省楚雄州的姚安、大姚等彝族地区。“梅葛”本为一种彝族歌调的名称，由于人们采用这种调子来唱彝族的创世史，因而创世史诗被称为“梅葛”。《查姆》是一部彝族史诗，是彝族人民唱天地、日月、人类、种子、风雨、树木等起源的长篇史诗，被彝族人民当作本民族的历史来看待。

其余几本书展示了一些少数民族的风俗习惯、恋爱故事、斗争故事等。《哭嫁歌》是土家族文化典籍。“哭嫁”是土家族姑娘在出嫁时进行的一种用歌声来诉说自己在封建买办婚姻制度下不幸命运的活动，是指土家族姑娘的抒情歌谣，富有诗韵和乐感，融哀、怨、喜和乐为一体，以婉转的曲调向世人展示土家人独特的“哭”文化。《彝族民间故事》是一部以流传于云南楚雄彝族自治州彝族人民中间的民间故事为主体，同时覆盖全省包括小凉山等彝族地区的民间故事集。这些故事丰富多彩，从中能看到民族民间故事的各种形态和生动、奇妙而颇具彝族民族特色的文化特征。《召树屯》是傣族民间长篇叙事诗，叙述了傣族佛教世俗典籍《贝叶经·召树屯》中一个古老的传说故事。这部叙事诗一直为傣族人民所传唱，历久不衰。《娥并与桑洛》是一部优美生动的叙事诗，一个凄美的爱情悲剧。《金笛》是一部苗族长篇叙事诗，富于变幻性和传奇性，尽情铺叙扎董丕冉与蒙诗彩奏的悲欢离合，热情赞颂他们在与魔虎的激烈斗争中所表现出来的坚贞不屈、英勇顽强的精神，许多情节含有浓郁的民族特色。

这些故事都很引人入胜，都很符合国家文化发展需求，向世人讲述中国故事，传播中华文化，并且讲述的是民族故事，充分体现了党和国家对各民族的关怀。

民族典籍英译是传播中国文化、文学和文明的重要途径，是中华文化“走出去”的重要组成部分，是国家战略，是提高文化“软实力”的重要方式，在文化交流和文明建设中起着不可或缺的作用，对提升中国国际话语权和构建中国对外话语体系以及对建设世界文学都有积极意义。

中国民族典籍使世界文化更加丰富多彩、绚丽多姿。我国各民族典籍中折射出的文化多样性极大地丰富了世界多元、特色鲜明的文化。人们对多样性形成全新的认识角度和思维方式，有助于开阔视野，丰富思考问题的角度，挖掘这些经典中的教育价值和文化价值，对世界其他民族都有指导和借鉴意义，并且有助于建设我国的文化自信。

民族典籍翻译与研究事业关乎国家的稳定统一，关乎民族关系的和谐发展，关乎世界多元文化的实现。在中国，民族典籍资源极为丰富，有待进一步挖掘、翻译，仍有许多少数民族典籍亟待拯救，民族典籍翻译与研究工作任重而道远，民族典籍翻译事业大有可为。

李正栓①

2019 年 7 月 19 日

① 李正栓，中国英汉语比较研究会典籍英译专业委员会常务副会长兼秘书长；中国中医药研究促进会传统文化翻译与国际传播专业委员会常务主任委员。

前　　言

在我国各民族的文学宝库中，傣族民间文学是一颗璀灿的明珠。傣族民间叙事长诗是傣族社会生活、人民心理素质和傣族风土人情的结晶。而爱情叙事长诗《召树屯》更是傣族民间文学中的瑰宝，其艺术表现手法造就了作品的不朽。它用神话手法刻画英雄，以爱情为主线反映社会生活，在正义与邪恶的对比中塑造人物。它不仅在我国的傣族地区，也在东南亚各国广为流传，很具代表性。

《召树屯》是一部傣族民间叙事长诗，也是一部佛教世俗典籍故事。数百年来，它一直为傣族人民所传唱，历久不衰。故事讲述了勐板加王子召树屯(意为勇敢的王子)出猎时在金湖与孔雀神女喃婼娜相爱，并结为夫妇。婚后不久便发生战争。召树屯出征后，摩古拉诬陷喃婼娜为不祥之物，欲杀之以祭神。喃婼娜要求临终一舞，于是得以飞返孔雀国勐董板。召树屯胜利归来不见爱妻，愤而追寻喃婼娜，历尽千辛万苦始达孔雀国，经过国王叭团的考验，夫妻终于团圆。

这部长诗由云南省少数民族古籍整理出版规划办公室整理、汉译，是翻译成汉文的第一部傣族文学作品。《召树屯》被整理、改编进入汉语文学圈，是 20 世纪中国文学的一大成就。本书由十二部分构成，分别为诗人的歌、王子召树屯、勐董板有七个姑娘、猎人、告别、爱情、拴线礼、战争、灾难、追赶、到了勐董板地方、团圆。十二部分环环相扣，动人地描述了召树屯与喃婼娜的忠贞爱情，反映了古代傣族人民的生活、思想与感情。

《召树屯》作为一部经典傣族叙事长诗，承载了少数民族璀璨的文化传统和历史精神，体现了傣族人民从自然界中吸取的经验和智慧。在翻译过程中，译者采用了异化、对等、文化补偿等翻译策略。异化、对等是为了最大限度地还原《召树屯》的文化内涵，促进少数民族文化的有效对外传播；文化补偿的目的在于解决文学翻译中的文化缺省问题。为了让跨文化读者理解文字背后的意义，译者采取了直译加注的方法，通过加注来具体说明背后的文化内涵和历史知识，以补充翻译过程中文化缺省的内容。

2008 年，《召树屯与喃木诺娜》①被列入第二批国家级非物质文化遗产名录，然而《召树屯》的英译及研究并未受到足够关注。希望本书的出版能为保护和传承傣族的非物质文化遗产奉献绵薄之力。

陈兰芳

2020 年 3 月于中南民族大学

① 此处《召树屯与喃木诺娜》即《召树屯》，西双版纳地区的傣族称为《召树屯》《召树屯与喃木诺娜》或《孔雀公主》。

目　　录

Contents

一、诗人的歌

太阳从树林里伸出头
呆呆地望着我写这个故事
公鸡也朝我扇开翅膀
我的故事正在金色的天空中飞翔

美丽的故事像一片艳丽的彩霞
纯洁的爱情就像并蒂开放的鲜花
真心相爱的青年人啊
请把这份礼物收下

我要用最诚实的心
描下他们的欢乐和痛苦
让我的歌啊
像一棵绿莹莹的菩提树

1. The Poet's Song

The sun is rising up from behind the woods
Staring at me as I write this story
The rooster also fans its wings at me
As my story is soaring in the golden sky

A beautiful story is like a flamboyant cloud
Pure love is like the blooming twin flowers
Ah, young people in true love
Please accept this gift

I want to use the most sincere heart
To depict the joy and pain of the young couple
Let my song
Rise like an emerald-colored bodhi tree①

① Bodhi tree, the tree of the Buddha, is significant in the history of Buddhism. It is a large and very old sacred fig tree located in Bodh Gaya (the birthplace of Buddhism), under which Siddhartha Gautama, the founder of Buddhism who later became known as the Buddha, is said to have attained enlightenment.

请四面八方飞来的鸟群
都停下翅膀
请会唱的“鹳托朗”①
绕着菩提树歌唱

从远方来的客人
带来他们的歌声
使各村各寨来的男女
带来他们的爱情

常青的菩提树啊
每一片叶子都是有情人的心
那蒙蒙的大雾啊
它夜夜来滋润

① “鹳托朗”：一种在夜里唱歌的鸟，声音婉转动人。

Birds flocking from all directions
Please fold your wings
"Otoran"①, the best of the songbirds
Please sing around the bodhi tree

Guests from afar
Bring their songs
Men and women from all villages
Bring their love

Ah, the evergreen bodhi trees
Each leaf belongs to a lover's heart
Ah, the misty fog
Moisturizes the trees night after night

① "Otoran": a bird which sings at night, agreeably and movingly.

二、王子召树屯

在古老的勐板加地方
住着皇后玛茜娜
她梦见老鹰落在屋顶上
过了十个月，生下了一个男孩

为了孩子的命运
国王请来了“摩古拉”①
摩古拉翻开了历书
在四十六个格子②里寻找幸福

“天空中最能飞的是老鹰
地上跑得最快的是金鹿
孩子的名字啊
应该叫做‘召树屯’③

---

① “摩古拉”：傣族卜卦算命的人。

② 四十六个格子：傣族卜卦算命的根据，在傣族经书中相传有四十六种野兽，前一种野兽管辖后一种。

③ 召树屯：坚强勇敢的王子。

2. Prince Zhaoshutun

In the ancient Mengbanjia①
Lived Queen Maxina
She dreamed one day that an eagle landed on the roof of her house
Ten months later, she gave birth to a son

For the future of the child
The king called for "Mogula"②
Who opened the almanac
Searching for happiness among the forty-six squares③

"The best in the sky is the eagle
The fastest on the ground is the golden stag
Ah, the child's name
Should be 'Zhaoshutun'④

---

① Mengbanjia: an ancient place in Yunnan Province, China.

② "Mogula": the soothsayer of the Dai nationality.

③ Forty-six squares: They are the basis on which soothsayers divine. There are forty-six wild animals ranked in a certain order, according to the Dai people. Those wild animals on higher ranks control those on lower ones.

④ Zhaoshutun: the determined and courageous prince.

"最好看的玉石常常有斑痕
生得最直的树容易遭受风吹雨淋
幸福的王子
他会遭到爱情的折腾"

十六年的幼苗长成树
十六年的召树屯长成英俊的青年
他的容貌像熔金般闪光
他的心肠像麂子般善良

他像一条神龙
在勐板加地方造下湖水
勐板加的百姓
就像开在湖里的金莲

英俊的召树屯
常常骑着马带着弩箭
在森林里追逐金鹿
在高空中射落飞雁

他也按照风俗
领着百姓赕佛①
祈求"灭巴拉"②
给勐板加带来风调雨顺

① 赕佛：献佛、敬佛之意。
② "灭巴拉"：管理雨水的神。

"The best jade often has markings
The most upright tree is likely to be exposed to wind and rain
The happy prince
He will suffer from the torment of love"

The seedling grew into a tree in sixteen years
And Zhaoshutun became a handsome young man
His looks were radiated with golden gleams
His heart was kind like that of a muntiacus

Like the magic dragon
He built a lake in Mengbanjia
People in Mengbanjia
Lived like the golden lotus in the lake

Handsome Zhaoshutun
Often rode around carrying with him his bolt
Hunting golden stags in the forest
Or flying geese in the sky

He also followed the customs
Leading people to worship the Buddha
And to pray to "Miebala" ①
To bring favorable weather to Mengbanjia

---

① Miebala: the rain god.

三、勐董板有七个姑娘

离勐板加很远很远
在那云雾缥缈之间
有一个奇妙的地方
它的名字叫勐董板

勐董板是个好地方
遍地开鲜花
满山是牛羊
来往的人都骑着大象

勐董板的国王叫作“叭团”①
他有七个一般大小的姑娘
她们像七只飞雁
披上孔雀的羽毛
就能在天空飞翔

① “叭团”：直译为魔鬼的头人，在此当“孔雀国王”解释。

3. The Seven Young Women in Mengdongban

Far away from Mengbanjia
In the midst of the misty clouds
There was a mysterious place
Its name was Mengdongban①

Mengdongban was a fine place
Where flowers were blooming everywhere
Mountains were full of cattle and sheep
And people travelled by riding elephants

The king of Mengdongban was called "Batuan"②
He had seven daughters of about the same age
Like seven flying geese
When they put on peacock feathers
They could fly in the sky

---

① Mengdongban: The Peacock State, which is the richest, the most beautiful and the best reigned state along the Lancang River.

② Batuan: the king of the Peacock State.

七个公主啊
七朵海棠
花中有花王
最鲜艳的花朵
要算喃婼娜——第七个姑娘

密密丛丛的树林里
有一个镜子般的金湖碧波荡漾
美丽的凤凰在那里栖息
多情的金鹿在望着水中的情郎

湖边有一座古寺
古寺里住着一个“叭拉纳西”①
他像蜜蜂一样日夜念经
古寺里的钟声悠悠扬扬

① “叭拉纳西”：据说是佛教传入中国初期在森林中修行的和尚。

Ah, the seven princesses
The seven begonias
Among them there was a queen
The most beautiful flower
Had to be Nanruona①—the seventh daughter.

In the dense woods
There was a mirror-like rippling lake
Beautiful phoenixes perched by it
And sensuous golden stags looked at themselves reflected in the water

By the lake was an ancient temple
Where lived a "Balanaxi"②
He chanted day and night like a bee
Accompanied by the resonance of the bell in the ancient temple

---

① Nanruona: the youngest Peacock Princess.

② Balanaxi: according to legends, they were monks who practiced Buddhism in the forest during the time when Buddhism was just introduced to China.

每隔七天
七个美丽的姑娘飞到湖边
每隔七天
湖边的花都为她们开放
雀鸟悄悄飞来偷看
只见千万层白花花的水浪中
七朵鲜花一晃一晃

Every seven days
Seven beautiful young women flew to the lakeside
Every seven days
The flowers bloomed for them
When the birds came stealthily to take a peek
They saw in the midst of thousands of layers of white waves
The seven fresh flowers① swaying back and forth

① The seven fresh flowers here refer to the seven Peacock Princesses who were swimming in the lake.

四、猎人

从竹林中跑出一个猎人
骑着马拿着弩箭
他追逐着一只金鹿
从树林里追到湖边

他忽然站在岸旁
就像拴牛的木桩
金鹿从他脚上奔过
他也没有看见

想吃鱼的翡翠鸟总是蹲在水边
蝙蝠一看见佛寺就绕着飞转①
年轻的猎人啊
他的眼睛就像两颗明珠
沉落在湖水中间

① “蝙蝠绕寺飞”是傣族成语，据传说，从前有一个和尚被头人赶出佛寺，无家可归，由于他怀念佛寺，后来变为一只蝙蝠绕着佛寺飞。

4. The Hunter

From the bamboo grove ran out a hunter
Riding a horse with his bolt in hand
He was chasing a golden stag
From the woods to the side of the lake

He suddenly stood by the shore
Like an ox post
The golden stag ran away right in front of him
But he was unaware of it

Halcyons that love fish always squat by the waterside
Bats on seeing a Buddhist temple fly around it①
Ah, the young hunter
His eyes were like two bright pearls
Fixed onto the middle of the lake

① "Bats on seeing a Buddhist temple fly around it" is a saying of the Dai people. It's said that a monk was driven away from the Buddhist temple and became homeless. However, he was nostalgic about the temple, so he became a bat always flying around the temple.

落日把他的影子送到水面
惊动了七朵浮莲
好像麻雀看见了老鹰
她们披起羽毛飞向远方

湖水又恢复了平静
鸟雀也飞回森林
只有猎人啊
还在呆呆望着青天

钟声突然把他惊醒
骏马呜呜嘶鸣
他揉一揉眼睛
便打马来到寺院

猎人跪在叭拉纳西的脚下
求他解开爱情的锁链
“都卑龙啊①
我不知道是在梦里，
还是真正活在人间

① “都卑龙”：直译为大佛爷。

The sunset projected his shadow onto the surface of the lake
And it startled the seven floating lotus flowers①
Like sparrows who saw an eagle
They put on the feathers and flew away

The peace was restored to the lake
And the birds returned to the forest
Only the hunter
Still stared blankly at the blue sky

The ringing of the bell suddenly awakened him from the trance
His horse neighing
He rubbed his eyes
And went with his horse to the temple

Kneeling at the feet of Balanaxi
The hunter prayed for the chain of love to be undone
"Ah, Dubeilong ②
I don't know whether I am in a dream
Or live in the real world

---

① The seven floating lotus flowers: the seven Peacock Princesses (a metaphor).

② Dubeilong: The literal translation is Master Buddha.

“我看见湖里有七个姑娘
像莲花一样发出清香
金色的带子装饰在头上
脖子上的珠宝闪烁发光

“可是，她们已经飞向天堂
美丽的天使啊
像彩虹使我眼晕
像老鹰叼去了我的心脏”

叭拉纳西问他是哪里来的猎人
他说他是勐板加的小王子
刚生下来的时候
大家就叫他召树屯

叭拉纳西眯起了眼睛
冷冷地笑了一声
召树屯哀求道：“请你不要笑我
我确确实实喜欢她们”

“青年人啊，你抬一抬头
这是佛寺，这是佛身
你还活在人间
就应该遵守人的本分

"I saw seven young women in the lake
They smelled like the lotus
Their heads decorated with golden ribbons
And their necks shimmering with jewelries

"But they have flown to the heavenly palace
Ah, beautiful angels
It feels like my eyes are dazzled by the rainbow
And my heart was stolen by an eagle"

Balanaxi asked where the hunter was from
He replied that he was the youngest prince of Mengbanjia
Since he was born
Everyone had called him Zhaoshutun

Balanaxi narrowed his eyes
Sneering
Zhaoshutun implored: "Please do not laugh at me
I really like them"

"Young man, look up and around
This is a Buddhist temple, the Buddha body
You still live in the world
And should abide by human obligations

"她们是天王的公主
她们是神仙的化身
世间从来就没有一条路
通到那个地方

"丢了你的梦想
你不是'锦那丽'①
你也没有'锦那暖'②的翅膀
就好像爬上树去捉鱼
就好像下到水里捞月亮"

猎人懊恼地拜别了叭拉纳西
像白天的猫头鹰飞出树林
他牵着马又来到金波荡漾的湖旁
用手轻轻拨起浪花
水波中又闪现出七朵红花

树影在水中晃动
七个姑娘对他微笑
慢慢朝他游浮
啊，那是红色的鱼在水中游弋

那是月亮和星星在湖中的光影
那是银河流向金湖

---

①② "锦那丽""锦那暖"：传说是两种飞得最快的鸟，每天飞绕大地七十七转。

"They are the heavenly king's princesses
The incarnation of the Immortals
There has never been a road in this world
That can connect to that place

"Abandon your dream
You are not 'Jinnali' ①
Nor do you have the wings of 'Jinnanuan'
Your dream is as silly as the idea of climbing a tree to catch fish
Or going down to the lake to fetch the moon"

The hunter bid farewell to Balanaxi, frustrated
Like an owl flying out of the woods during the day
He led his horse and returned to the lake with the golden ripples
Gently stirring up the spray by hand
He saw the seven red flowers flashing in the water

The shadows of the trees were wavering in the water
And the seven young women were smiling at him
Drifting slowly towards him
Ah, they were red fish cruising in the water

It was the reflection of the moon and the stars in the lake
It was the Milky Way flowing into the Golden Lake

---

① "Jinnali" and "Jinnanuan": two kinds of birds that fly the fastest. It's said that every day they could fly around the earth seventy-seven times.

那是神龙带领着虾兵蟹将
在他的湖中巡行

“神龙啊，你是我的好朋友
我曾经救过你的生命①
如今我遇到困难
你能不能给我帮助”

神龙浮出水面
张开嘴哈哈大笑
“我的朋友呀
什么风把你刮到这里

“是病魔纠缠着你
还是有人来攻打勐板加
你是我的救命恩人
我一定为你效命”

猎人诉出了心中的苦恼
神龙又是一阵爽朗的大笑
接着就把七个姑娘的秘密
对召树屯讲了

① 传说召树屯在金湖边狩猎时看见一只老鹰将神龙叼入空中，召树屯用箭射死老鹰，救了神龙，后来他和神龙结为朋友。

It was the magic dragon leading its shrimp soldiers and crab generals①
Patrolling the lake

"Ah, magic dragon, you are my good friend
I once saved your life②
Now that I have encountered difficulties
Could you help me, please"

The magic dragon rose to the surface
Bursting into laughter
"My dear friend
What brought you here

"Is it the disease that is haunting you
Or the enemy who is attacking Mengbanjia
You're my rescuer
And I'm at your service"

When the hunter explained the anguish in his heart
The magic dragon burst into hearty laughter again
He then told Zhaoshutun
The secrets of the seven young women

① Shrimp soldiers and crab generals appear in Chinese mythology or popular fiction, referring to the army of the Dragon King of the Eastern Sea.

② It's said that while hunting along the golden lake, Zhaoshutun found an eagle carrying the magic dragon off to the sky. He shot the eagle and rescued the dragon, which thereafter became his friend.

五、告别

召树屯按照神龙的话
用长刀砍了许多竹子
在大树上搭起了竹棚
他就躲在那里等候

过了一天又一天
月亮在湖里洗了七次脸
凤凰飞来饮了七次水
召树屯在湖边等了七天七夜

那一天无风无云
蓝空里飞来七只孔雀
她们轻轻地落在湖边
又像花一样飘落到水面

笑声泛起波纹
花朵飘向湖心
召树屯悄悄爬到湖岸
拿走了喃婼娜的孔雀衣

5. Farewell

Following the magic dragon's advice
Zhaoshutun cut down a lot of bamboo with his long knife
And built a bamboo shed on the tree
There he hid and waited

One day passed, and then another
The moon washed its face in the lake seven times
The phoenix came to drink water seven times
And Zhaoshutun waited by the lake for seven days and seven nights

It was a windless and cloudless day
When seven peacocks flew in from the blue sky
They landed softly by the lake
And then on the surface of the lake, like floating flowers

Their laughter caused the ripples
As the flowers drifted towards the middle of the lake
Zhaoshutun quietly crept to the shore
And took away Nanruona's peacock clothes

召树屯回到了竹棚
便放声歌唱
七个姑娘慌忙回到岸上
喃婼娜不见了衣裳

没有翅膀的鸟不会飞
没有鱼鳍的鱼不会游水
没有衣裳的喃婼娜
无法向天空追她的姐妹

歌声越来越近
喃婼娜慌忙躲进花丛
喃婼娜的手啊
被谁轻轻地牵动

六只孔雀在空中徘徊
她们看见猎人拉住了妹妹
像有六支箭射进她们的心中
像有六把刀砍在她们的身上

十二只翅膀
一齐扑向猎人
六个姐姐的头
一齐冲向召树屯

Zhaoshutun returned to the bamboo shed
Singing aloud
The seven young women hurried back to the shore
But Nanruona couldn't find her clothes

Birds without wings cannot fly
Fish without fins cannot swim
Without her clothes, Nanruona
Was unable to chase her sisters into the sky

The sound of the singing was getting closer
Nanruona hid hurriedly in the blossoms
Ah, Nanruona's hand
Was gently held by a person

The six peacocks were hovering in the sky
Seeing the hunter holding their younger sister's hand
It was like six arrows shooting into their hearts
Like six knives stabbing into their bodies

Twelve wings
Swooped down together on the hunter
Six heads of the sisters
Charged together at Zhaoshutun

情人不会吐掉嘴里的槟榔①
姑娘不会轻易拔下头上的金簪
召树屯不愿放走心爱的喃婼娜
六个姐姐的眼泪
雨滴般洒在湖上

“再见啊，可怜的喃婼娜
我们向你告别了
要是以前我们做错了什么事
妹妹呵，请你原谅我们

“当我们飞下来的时候
我们总是把你围在中间
现在你竟被猎人捉去
这一切都是命中注定

“我们赶回去告诉爹妈
阿妈会很伤心
阿妈会请求阿爹
赶快派兵来救你”

① 傣族青年男女在互相恋爱时，常用槟榔来款待情人。傣族人认为吃了槟榔的人不会变心。

Lovers won't spit areca nuts① in their mouths
Girls won't easily remove the gold hairpins in their hair
Zhaoshutun would not let go of his beloved Nanruona
Six sisters' tears
Sprinkled like raindrops on the lake

"Good-bye, poor Nanruona
We bid farewell to you
If we have done something wrong before
Please forgive us, our sister

"Whenever we flew down
We always kept you in the middle
Now you are caught by a hunter
All this is fate

"We will hurry back to inform dad and mum
Mum will be sad
And will plead with dad
To send troops to rescue you"

---

① Areca nut: It's the seed of the betel palm. In southeastern Asia, people chew it with the leaves of the betel pepper and lime as a digestive stimulant and as a narcotic. When Dai young people fall in love, they often entertain each other with areca nuts, and it is believed that doing so can help them remain faithful to each other.

喃婼娜的眼睛望着天空
眼泪遮住了姐姐们的身影
她低下头说不出话
只向姐姐们“合掌”①

“从今以后
我们恐怕不能相见
请把我的话转告父母和头人
喃婼娜啊
永远想念他们”

① “合掌”：傣族的一种礼节，表示对对方的尊敬和诚意。

Nanruona was looking at the sky
Tears blocked her sight of her sisters
She lowered her head and could not speak
Only to "put her palms together"① to her sisters

"From now on
I'm afraid we won't see each other again
Please tell our parents and the headman
Ah, Nanruona
Will always miss them"

① "Put one's palms together": It is a custom of the Dai people to show respect and sincerity to others.

六、爱情

湖水一片平静
喃婼娜微微打战
就像风雨飘到她的身上
她不知道猎人将对她怎样

召树屯轻轻脱下自己的衣裳
把它披在喃婼娜的身上
然后他跪在姑娘的面前
嘴里又轻轻歌唱

“美丽的姑娘啊
我像一只粗野的狼
我像无礼的暴君
我的心啊，像金鹿一样善良

“请雪白的云朵给我作证
请微风表白我的心肠
粉团花啊

6. Love

The lake was peaceful
Nanruona trembled slightly
It felt like the wind and the rain falling on her
She didn't know how the hunter would treat her

Zhaoshutun gently took off his clothes
And put it on Nanruona
He then knelt before the young woman
And sang softly

"Beautiful young woman
I look like a rough wolf
I acted like an impudent tyrant
But my heart is as kind as a golden deer

"Let the snow-white clouds be my witness
And let the gentle breeze express my heart
Ah, hydrangea flower

我只是一只平常的蜜蜂

“请你不要再用双手遮住脸
只求你轻轻看我一眼
我知道，只要你看我一眼
你就会看清我的心房”

喃婼娜依然一声不响
就像含羞草被人触动
她的眼睛啊
像天上的星星闪烁

椰子树没有他英俊
十五的月亮比不上他的眼睛
哪里来的小伙子呀
菠萝的滋味
也比不上他的歌声

召树屯恨不得拔出长刀
掏出自己的心房
他不知道该用什么办法
才能表白他的爱恋与敬仰

I'm just a common bee①

"Please remove your hands that are covering your face
Just take a glance at me
I know that one look at me
Will show you my heart"

Nanruona was still silent
Like a mimosa having just been touched by a person
But, ah, her eyes
Were twinkling like the stars in the sky

The coconut tree was not as handsome as him
The full moon was not as bright as his eyes
Where came this young man
The taste of pineapples
Was no match for his song

Zhaoshutun wished to pull out his long knife
To take out his heart
He didn't know how
To express his love and admiration

① Ah, hydrangea flower, I'm just a common bee: hydrangea flower is a species of flowering plant which bears large conical panicles of creamy white fertile flowers, together with pinkish white sterile florets. In the language of flowers, it represents hope, loyalty, eternity, reunion and a happy marriage. Here Zhaoshutun bares his heart to Nanruona.

“多兰嘎①啊
请你打开谷仓
请你把爱情的种籽
播在姑娘的心上

“姑娘啊
我不是狐狸
不会吃小鸡
我不是老虎
不会伤害人

“我是勐板加的一只丑鸭
我是猎人的一支秃箭
我是田野上能望的鹭鸶②
我的名字叫做召树屯”

喃婼娜听见这个名字
不觉吃了一惊
摩古拉曾经说过
她将嫁给一个勇敢善良的人
她的心里暗暗喜欢
恰恰遇到了心上的人

① 多兰嘎：傣族传说中的爱神。

② 相传，鹭鸶与孔雀恋爱，因孔雀飞进森林里，鹭鸶等待孔雀，脖子都望长了。

"Ah, Duolanga①
Please open your barn
Please take the seeds of love
And spread them on the heart of this young woman

"Ah, young woman
I'm not a fox
And I won't eat chicken
I am not a tiger
I won't hurt people

"I am an ugly duck from Mengbanjia
I am a bald arrow of the hunter
I am an egret in the field that is on the tiptoe of expectation②
My name is Zhaoshutun"

On hearing this name
Nanruona was taken aback
Mogula once said
She would marry a brave and kind man
Secretly, she started to become fond of him
She had met her beloved

---

① Duolanga: the god of love in the Dai legends.

② An egret in the field that is on the tiptoe of expectation: It's said that an egret fell in love with a peacock. Later, the peacock left and went into the forest, and the egret waited for the peacock till its neck became long.

召树屯的眼睛没有离开过喃婼娜
召树屯的嘴没有停止歌声
在喃婼娜没有对他回答之前
他决心一辈子歌唱不停

“可爱的姑娘啊
请打开你的心扉
不管天崩地裂
鱼啊，只有在水里才能生存

“我只要每天看见你一眼
没有吃的我也心甘
请你这朵花开在我园里
让我变成浇花的水”

母鸡听见公鸡叫唤会扇开翅膀
召树屯的歌声
像一只蜜蜂落在喃婼娜的心上
她望着湖水
又羞又喜地低声歌唱

“热辣辣的太阳
会使鲜花枯萎
你过热的爱情啊
叫我的心跳荡

Zhaoshutun's eyes never left Nanruona
And he did not stop singing
Before Nanruona responded to him
He was determined to sing nonstop for the rest of his life

"Ah, lovely young woman
Please open your heart
Even if heaven fell and earth crumbled
Fish, ah, they can only survive in the water

"As long as I can see you once every day
I will be willing to go hungry
Please be the flower in my garden
And let me become the water for the flower"

The hen would fan its wings on hearing the cock crow
The sound of Zhaoshutun's song
Like a bee touched Nanruona's heart
She looked at the lake
And sang shyly and joyously in a low voice

"The scorching sun
Could wither the flowers
Ah, your overheated love
Makes my heart beat fast

"一棵芭蕉只结一次果
懂得修剪花蕊的人啊
芭蕉果会愈结愈多

"一棵香瓜只抽一次藤
会种香瓜的人啊
一棵香瓜爬满瓜棚

"愿你像一棵椰子树
树高根深
我会天天坐在树下
觉得快活凉爽"

召树屯的两颊发烫
心里像煮开的水一样
他站起身
放声歌唱

"姑娘啊
你的歌声像湖里的清水
让我洗了一次澡
姑娘啊
只有现在，我才感到
我是一个骄傲的国王

"A banana tree bears fruit only once
But those who know how to prune flowers
Can make their trees bear more and more bananas

"A muskmelon seedling grows vines only once
But those who know how to plant muskmelons
Can produce from one plant vines that cover the whole shed

"May you be a coconut tree
With tall trunk and deep roots
I will sit under the tree every day
Feeling happy and cool"

Zhaoshutun's cheeks were burning
His heart felt like boiling water
He rose
And sang loudly

"Ah, young woman,
Your song is like the clear water in the lake
That has just cleansed me
Ah, young woman
It is only now that I feel
I am a proud king

“姑娘啊
你看见没有
湖边的花为我们开放
林中的鸟也为我们歌唱”

召树屯轻轻拉起喃婼娜
一对情侣沿着湖岸
像凤凰一样漫舞低唱

"Ah, young woman
Did you see
That the flowers on the lakeside have blossomed for us
And the birds in the woods are also singing for us"

Zhaoshutun gently held Nanruona's hand
The lovers went along the lakeshore
Like two phoenixes dancing freely and singing softly

七、拴线礼[①]

走出重重的森林
眼前是一片平坦的坝子
落日赶着成群的牛羊
村寨在彩霞中闪亮

召树屯指着坝子说
“看啊，喃婼娜
这就是我们的家乡
这就是我们的勐板加地方”

喃婼娜朝着召树屯指的方向眺望
一千间房子镶着金边
一万根栋梁雕刻了龙身
墙上画满了花草和飞鸟

喘息的马儿
扬起了灰尘

① 拴线礼：傣族的一种仪式，在祝贺结婚或为新生婴儿免除灾难的时候，都举行拴线礼，通常是由年长的人将一根红线拴在被祝贺人的手上，表示吉祥。

7. Thread Tying Ceremony[①]

Out of the dense forest
Emerged in the horizon a flatland
Herds of cattle and sheep seemed as if driven by the sunset
And villages were shining in the rosy clouds

Zhaoshutun pointed to the flatland and said
"Ah, Look, Nanruona
This is our hometown
This is our Mengbanjia"

Nanruona looked at where Zhaoshutun was pointing
One thousand houses were rimmed with gold
Ten thousands beams were carved with dragons
The walls were painted with plants and flying birds

The panting horse
Kicked up the dust

---

① Thread tying ceremony: It's a ceremony of the Dai nationality to celebrate marriages or newborns. It is usually the elderly person that ties a red thread on the wrists of the couple to symbolize auspiciousness.

穿过田野
他们来到了城边

一阵咚咚的鼓声
召来了许多百姓
他们是来看喃婼娜
他们是来迎接召树屯

人们都赞赏喃婼娜的美丽
“这是一朵正要开放的腊梅花
勐板加地方
找不出这样一个美女”

召树屯把喃婼娜带回家里
头人和百姓都在议论
赶快给他们“拴线”
有的人给喃婼娜准备金伞
有人去准备“喃菩他”圣水①

全勐的百姓都来庆贺
他们送来了蜡条②
送酒的人像一条河

① “喃菩他”圣水：七种金属粉混起来的溶液，传说用来洗澡，可以得到吉祥。

② 蜡条：用黄蜡做成的细条，可以点燃，象征吉祥。

Once having crossed the field
They arrived at the outside of the city

A burst of drums
Attracted many people
They came to meet Nanruona
They came to welcome back Zhaoshutun

People all admired the beauty of Nanruona
"This is a plum bud ready to blossom
In Mengbanjia
We cannot find such a beauty"

Zhaoshutun brought Nanruona home
Headman and people were saying
Hurry and do the "thread tying ceremony"
Some prepared a golden umbrella for Nanruona
Others went to get ready the holy water of "Nanputa"①

Everyone in Mengbanjia came to celebrate
They brought wax bars②
The line of people offering wine was long like a river

---

① "Nanputa": It's a solution made up of seven kinds of metal powder. It's said that if you have a bath with it, you will be blessed with auspiciousness.

② Wax bars: bars made up of yellow wax, which can be lit up to symbolize auspiciousness.

村村寨寨都为他们赶猪赶羊

宫殿里响起三声大炮
象脚鼓、芒锣一起敲响
百姓像朝王的蜜蜂
唱着、跳着涌进皇宫

一群侍女捧着蜡条跟着喃婼娜
来到大厅里，便一个个跪下
召树屯燃起蜡条走到她的身边
年老的阿爹手上拿了一根红线
轻轻地拴在他们的手上
又把蜡条吹熄

阿妈把他们扶到门边
大象把前腿跪在他们面前
召树屯和喃婼娜骑上大象
绕着村寨游了一圈

沿路都是百姓
跪在地上为他们滴水①
嘴里为他们祝福
孩子们都喊着“水！水！水！”②

① 滴水：用水滴在地上，是一种祝福的仪式。
② “水！水！水！”：欢呼声。

Every village sent pigs and sheep to them①

The palace cannons sounded three times
Xiangjiaogu and gongs were playing at the same time
People were like bees worshiping the queen
Singing and dancing, they poured into the palace

A group of maids held the wax bars and followed Nanruona
Arriving at the hall, they knelt down one by one
Zhaoshutun lit a wax bar and walked up to her side
Old father took a red thread
Tied gently to their wrists
And then blew out the wax bar

Mother helped them to get to the door
An elephant knelt down by its forelegs in front of them
Zhaoshutun and Nanruona mounted on the elephant
And went around the village once

People waited along the road
Kneeling on the ground, dripping water for them②
And giving them their blessings
Children shouted "Water! Water! Water!"③

① Sent pigs and sheep: In the Dai culture, when the headman gets married, people are supposed to send pigs and sheep as gifts.

② Dripping water for them: It's a blessing ceremony to drip water on the ground.

③ "Water! Water! Water! ": the sound of cheers.

转眼就到了七月
许多果树都开花了
喃婼娜和召树屯
开始收割他们的爱情

In a trice it was July
Many fruit trees were in blossom
Nanruona and Zhaoshutun
Started to harvest the fruit of their love

八、战争

六个姐姐啊
像带箭的鸟儿飞回到勐董板
跌跌爬爬来到爹妈面前
她们哭泣得说不成声
把爹妈吓得心神不定

“爹妈啊
喃婼娜遭到了不幸
猎人把她捉去
如今生死不明”

突然来的雷鸣
叫人胆破心惊
突然来的消息
害得老妈妈昏迷不醒

六个女儿救起了老母亲
千万支箭射中了叭团的心
他一声不响
眼泪淌得泉水一样不停

8. The War

The six sisters
Flew back to Mengdongban like birds shot by arrows
Staggering, they came before their father and mother
They were sobbing so much that they could hardly speak
And their father and mother were frightened into grave anxieties

"Oh dad and mum
Nanruona suffered a misfortune
A hunter captured her
We don't know whether she is dead or alive"

The unexpected thunder
Can be very scary
This sudden news
Shocked the old mother into a stupor

While the six daughters rescued their old mother
Batuan felt as if his heart was shot by thousands of arrows
He did not say anything
Tears running nonstop like a spring

喃婼娜是他们最小的姑娘
喃婼娜是他们掌上的明珠
喃婼娜是他们的心肝
喃婼娜从来没有离开过他们

喃婼娜的撒娇叫爹妈喜欢
喃婼娜的声音叫爹妈温暖
喃婼娜是家里的一只小鸟
只要她在家，人人都会快活

老妈妈从昏死中苏醒
她的眼泪哗哗流下
她的心像被撕成几片
她的声音像一根线的“琴”①

“可怜的喃婼娜啊
不幸的姑娘
你在那里受难
哪个能够救你回家

“晚上有哪个给你铺床
哪个来代你睡在我的身旁
你啊，怎么忍心丢下阿妈
叫我怎样活下去……”

---

① “琴”是傣族的一种乐器，类似二胡。傣族青年男女常常用琴传达感情。

Nanruona was their youngest daughter
Nanruona was the pearl in their palms
Nanruona was their sweetheart
Nanruona had never left them before

Nanruona pleased her parents even when acting pouty
Nanruona's voice warmed their hearts
Nanruona was a little bird of the family
As long as she was at home, everyone was cheerful

Mother woke up from fainting
Her tears streamed down
Her heart was torn into pieces
Her voice was like an "urhheen"① with only one string

"Poor Nanruona
The unlucky girl
You are suffering there
Who can get you home

"Who will make the bed for you at night
Who will sleep by my side instead of you
How could you leave your mom
How can I survive without you..."

① Urhheen: a musical instrument used by people of the Dai Nationality, with which boys and girls often convey their emotions.

母亲再也哭不出声
叭团猛地站起身
他击起大鼓
下令立刻出兵

在勐板加地方
召树屯和喃婼娜正过着好时光
芒锣和大鼓突然齐响
竹楼都被震得摇晃

灾难来到了勐板加
勐板加人心惶惶
召树屯传下命令
勇敢的人都挂上刀枪

骑马的来到召树屯面前
骑象的集中在广场
他们摩拳擦掌
人啊，像被暴风吹打的树林一样

召树屯穿上全副盔甲
默默来到妻子面前
向喃婼娜轻轻告别
“亲爱的喃婼娜
我们的日子刚开始
就遇到了不幸
不过，请你放心
我一定不会让你受惊

Mother cried till she couldn't make a voice any more
Batuan suddenly got to his feet
He hit the big drum
And ordered the troops to set out immediately

In Mengbanjia
Zhaoshutun and Nanruona were having a good time
Suddenly, the gongs and the drums rang
And the bamboo house began to shake

Disaster befell Mengbanjia
And people there were terrified
Zhaoshutun sent the command
That all brave men be armed with swords and guns

The horsemen came in front of Zhaoshutun
The elephant riders assembled at the square
People were gearing up
Ah, they looked like the forest trees hit by a storm

Dressed in full armor
Zhaoshutun quietly came to his wife
He bid farewell to her gently
"Dear Nanruona
Our good life has just started
And now this happens
But I assure you
I'll not let you be scared

“大树倒了会惊散鸟群
灾难会伤害人的生命
我啊，不能不离开心爱的人
但是，我的心将永远在你身边

“我知道
没有弦的琴
弹不出声音
看不见的雷声
却总是跟着闪电”

好梦常被风雨惊醒
喃诺娜的心里闪着霹雳
两股泪水淌过脸上
她低声对着丈夫唱吟

“你的爱情像血液一样
永远激荡着我的心房
在你的面前
就像在冬天的火塘旁

“请你不要为我伤心
请你不要为我怕去打仗
你的妻子
一万年都是为你活着

"The big tree fell and can startle the birds
Disasters can cause the loss of lives
Ah, I have to leave you, my beloved
But my heart will always be with you

"I know
That an urhheen without string
Cannot give out sound
But the invisible thunder
Always follows the lightning"

Like sweet dreams that are often disrupted by the storm
Nanruona's heart was shocked by thunderbolts
With two streams of tears running down her face
She sang to her husband in a low voice

"Your love is like blood
That is always pumping through my heart
Standing in front of you
I feel like I am by the fire pit in the winter

"Please do not be sad for me
Please do not be afraid of fighting because of me
Your wife
In ten thousand years will still live for you

"你要很好地带领那些勇士
不要让他们斜着眼睛看你
他们都是正直的人
他们会帮助你杀退仇敌

"我在家里
会用最真诚的心
祈求神灵帮助你
你会感觉到
你的妻子随时都站在你身旁

"去啊，不要说时间长
椰子要十年才会结果
葵花总是向着太阳
你一定会得胜
欢乐的日子会像青松一样"

喃婼娜说完话
又亲了亲他的头巾
召树屯便走出城门
大象已经来到他面前

他带领着八万人马
浩浩荡荡绕过田坝
穿过密密的森林
向边界出发

"Go lead those warriors
Do not let them look down upon you
They're all honest people
They will help you to kill or stop the enemy

"I will stay at home
With the most sincere heart
I will pray to the spirits to help you
You will feel
That your wife is standing by your side at all times

"Go, do not say it is a long time
Coconut takes ten years to bear fruit
Sunflowers always face the sun
You will prevail
And happy days will be like the evergreen pines"

With these words
Nanruona kissed his scarf
Zhaoshutun went out of the city gate
The elephant had come before him

He led eighty thousand troops
Went around the fields in a formidable array
Through dense forest
And set out to the border

九、灾难

召树屯离开了家乡
灾难就落在喃婼娜身上

有一个晚上
召树屯的阿爹做了一个梦
梦见他的肠子从肚子里飞出
绕着城池转了三转

他坐着肠子
像乘着飞龙在上空游转
然后肠子又回到他的身上

他被怪梦惊醒
一直呆坐到天亮
是凶是吉
叫他十分忐忑不安

他把所有的摩古拉都请来
那个最大的摩古拉掐指一算
脸色就发白
话到舌尖又吞了回去

9. Disaster

No sooner did Zhaoshutun leave his hometown
Than the disaster fell on Nanruona

One night
Zhaoshutun's dad had a dream
He dreamt of his intestines flying out of his stomach
And then revolving around the city three times

He sat on the intestines
Like riding a flying dragon in the sky
Before the intestines returned back to his body

He was awakened by the strange dream
And sat frozen with horror until dawn
Was it for good or ill
He felt quite uneasy

He invited all Mogulas
As soon as the supreme Mogula calculated with his fingers
His face turned pale
The words came to the tip of his tongue but he bit them back

什么事情使摩古拉作难
什么事情叫摩古拉不敢抬头
经过国王再三请求
摩古拉才说出口

“灾难就要像火一样燃烧
只因为你家里有了妖气
一棵树结不出两种果子
喃婼娜生得再漂亮
也不能和人住在一起”

国王愕然抬起头
半信半疑地望着摩古拉
他要摩古拉再三推算

摩古拉把头低下
装做诚心诚意
掐着指头算了又算
他皱起眉毛眯起了眼睛
嘴里吐出了骇人的字眼

“只有杀了喃婼娜
用她的血来祭百姓的神
才能消除百姓的灾难
才能叫你重生”

What put Mogula in such a dilemma
What made Mogula be afraid to raise his head
After the king's repeated requests
Mogula finally said it

"The disaster is about to burn like fire
Because of the evil spirit in your family
A tree cannot bear two kinds of fruit
Despite Nanruona's breathtaking beauty
She can't live with people"

The king looked up in astonishment
And looked at Mogula in disbelief
He urged Mogula to try again

Mogula lowered his head
Pretending to be sincere
He pinched his fingers and calculated repeatedly
With his brows knitted and his eyes narrowed
He uttered these terrible words

"Only when you kill Nanruona
And use her blood as sacrifice to the gods of the people
Can you eliminate the disaster of the people
And hope for your own reincarnation"

国王想了又想
既然是妖气就要除根
他问摩古拉
她该死在什么时辰

摩古拉烧起香火
庄严地宣布
“她将死在龙日
太阳刚刚上升的时刻”

时刻到了
乌云像青纱盖住太阳
勐板加一片阴暗、凄凉
百姓围在宫殿门前
眼睛都黯然无光

喃婼娜被叫唤出来
她脸上绯红、满怀高兴
以为百姓聚集门前
是来迎接丈夫得胜回转

当国王向她诉说真情
就像魔鬼撕碎了她的心
她几次昏倒又几次苏醒
跪在国王的面前哀哀求情

The king thought it over
And decided that the evil spirit must be eradicated
He asked Mogula
When she was supposed to die

Mogula burned some incense
And solemnly announced
"She will die on the dragon day
And at the moment of sunrise"

When that time came
Dark clouds like black gauze covered the sun
Mengbanjia was gloomy and sad
People assembled in front of the palace
With their eyes dull with no light

Nanruona was called out
Her face was crimson, full of pleasure
Thinking that people gathered in front of the palace
To welcome her husband to return victoriously

When the king told her the truth
She felt like her heart were shredded into pieces by the demon
She fainted several times and then awakened
Kneeling before the king and begging for her life

"阿爹啊
我本来是天上的一只神鸟
因为和你的儿子有缘
才从天上飞来

"我不会给你们带来灾难
求你不要听信谗言
只有阿爹的保护
暗箭才射不中我的身

"请你为你尊贵的儿子想一想
当他得胜回来
看不见心爱的妻子
他的心将会碎裂

"阿爹啊
没有水的树不会发芽
没有伴的雁啊
会伤心而死"

国王不敢抬眼去看喃婼娜
他只说："不杀你
勐板加就会遭难
召树屯也不能回转"

喃婼娜脸色苍黄
她的心像风中的布旗一样飘荡
她又向百姓求情
百姓都低头无声

"My dad
I used to be a divine bird in the sky
Because your son and I were predestined to be together
I came from the sky

"I will not bring you disaster
Please do not listen to the slander
Only with dad's protection
Can I shelter from the hidden arrows

"Please think about your noble son
When he returns triumphantly
But can no longer see his beloved wife
His heart will be broken

"Oh, dad
A tree without water will not sprout
A wild goose without a companion
Will die of grief"

The king dared not look at Nanruona
He just said: "If I don't kill you
Mengbanjia will suffer and
Zhaoshutun cannot return"

Nanruona's face turned sallow
Her heart felt like a flag fluttering in the wind
She then appealed to the people
But all the people lowered their heads in silence

喃婼娜十分伤心
脸上流下两行眼泪
她把头低下
等待死的时辰

死的时刻已将来临
她对阿妈告别
她说："阿妈啊，
我的命运既然是这样
我也只有听从

"召树屯回来的时候
请你为我向他告别
倒了的松树还有根
枯了的青草还会再生"

阿妈洒下了伤心泪
走向前去轻轻抚摸喃婼娜的头发
问喃婼娜还有什么话说

喃婼娜擦干了眼泪
她说："我是从舞蹈的地方飞来
当我临死的时刻
我只有一个请求

"请求把我的羽毛还给我
让我最后跳一次舞
再享一次人生的欢乐

Nanruona was so sad that
With two streams of tears running down her face
She lowered her head
Waiting to die

The moment of death had come,
She bid farewell to her mother-in-law
Saying, "Mum, since this is my destiny
I have to obey

"When Zhaoshutun comes back
Please say goodbye to him for me
The fallen pine tree still has roots
The withered grass will regenerate"

Mum shed tears of sadness
She went up to caress Nanruona's hair gently
And asked her what else she wanted to say

Nanruona wiped away her tears
And said, "I flew from the dancing place
Before I die
I have only one request

"Please return my feathers to me
And let me dance one last time
To enjoy the joy of life once more

我会安心地离开人世”

国王看了一看百姓
所有的眼睛都好像说
“人就要死了
国王应该答应”

阿妈怯生生地抱出了孔雀衣
喃婼娜接过来穿在身上
她拜了拜阿妈
就轻轻起舞

她抬起头向四面张望
四面都围满了百姓
看过一个一个脸孔
就是不见召树屯

她向百姓拜别
然后飞向屋顶
当她的脚离开了土地
眼泪像点点细雨

“阿爹阿妈啊，再见
头人们啊，再见
百姓们啊，再见
勐板加啊，再见

So that I can leave this world in peace"

The king looked at the people
All the eyes seemed to say
"She is at death's door
And the king should agree"

Mum timidly brought out the coat of peacock features
Nanruona took it and put it on
She bowed low to mum
And danced gently

She raised her head to look around
And found herself surrounded by people
She looked at the faces one by one
But couldn't find Zhaoshutun

She bid farewell to the people
And flew to the roof
When her feet left the land
Her tears were like rain drops drizzling down

"Goodbye, mum and dad
Goodbye, headmen
Goodbye, my people
Goodbye, Mengbanjia

“愿你们都过好日子
愿你们万寿无疆
愿勐板加地方啊
五谷丰收，遍地牛羊

“再见啊，我住过的房屋
再见啊，我走过的小路
再见啊，亲爱的城市
再见啊，召树屯的家乡

“请将我的话转告主人
我就要飞回勐董板
要是他怀念我的时候
就找一找别的姑娘吧

“千万请他把我忘记
我是一只无情的鸟
我就要飞回勐董板
勐董板是在另一个世界”

喃婼娜展开翅膀
她穿过云层飞向远方
不久，她又飞转回来
在勐板加上空盘旋

"My good wishes for you all to have a good life
To live long and prosper
For Mengbanjia
To have a bumper harvest with cattle and sheep everywhere

"Goodbye, the house I have lived in
Goodbye, the paths I have trodden
Goodbye, my dear city
Goodbye, Zhaoshutun's hometown

"Please convey my words to the master
I'm flying back to Mengdongban
If he misses me
Just find another young woman

"Do ask him to forget about me
I'm a cold-hearted bird
I'm going to fly back to Mengdongban
Which is in another world"

Nanruona spread her wings
And flew through the clouds to the far distance
But soon she flew back
Circling over Mengbanjia

她又向勐板加告别
但是她的头依旧不断回转
仿佛她掉落了东西
仿佛她忘记了金簪

喃婼娜飞来飞去
又停在一棵黄金果树上
森林里所有的鸟都飞来朝拜
她又渴又累，昏昏欲睡

鸟儿在四面歌唱
喃婼娜一惊
好像看见召树屯
啊，不，这是召树屯在怀念……

她匆匆飞起
又飞回到金湖边
最初的爱恋
又涌现在她眼前

她再没有力量远飞
两眼只是呆呆地望着湖水
夜雾的冷气把她惊醒
她才慢慢走到佛寺

She bid farewell to Mengbanjia again
But her head kept turning back
As if she had dropped something
As if she had forgotten her gold hairpin

Nanruona flew back and forth
And then stopped on a golden fruit tree
All the birds in the forest came to worship her
She was thirsty, tired and drowsy

The birds started singing around her
Nanruona was startled
As if she had seen Zhaoshutun
Ah, no, it was the yearning of Zhaoshutun...

She took off in a hurry
And returned to the side of the golden lake
The love at the very beginning
Reappeared before her eyes

She had no strength to fly anymore
Eyes just staring at the lake
Awakened by the frosty night air
She slowly walked to the Buddhist temple

她拜见了叭拉纳西
要求借宿一夜
叭拉纳西问她从哪里来
是不是从天上来到人间

“我不是出来游玩
我的丈夫是召树屯
只因为他去打仗
灾难降落到我的身上

“如果我的丈夫来到
请你劝他不要去寻找
前面没有人走的道路
野兽到处都会吃人

“请把这个金手镯转给他
要是他怀念我
请他问一问金手镯”

第二天一早
喃婼娜又从佛寺飞起
穿过森林和云彩
飞向自己的家乡

She paid a visit to Balanaxi
Asking for a night's lodging
Balanaxi asked where she came from
Whether she came from heaven to the world

"I am not out to play
My husband is Zhaoshutun
Just because he went to the war
Disaster fell on me

"If my husband comes
Please persuade him not to look for me
There's no path ahead for men to go
While there are man-eating beasts everywhere

"Please give this gold bracelet to him
If he misses me
Tell him to ask the gold bracelet"

Early next morning
Nanruona flew from the Buddhist temple
Crossing the forests and clouds
She flew towards her hometown

十、追赶

战争已经胜利结束
勐板加的百姓热热闹闹
吹起金号银号
迎接自己的亲人

召树屯在人群中
找寻自己的妻子
喃婼娜啊
为什么不见你出来欢迎

为什么看不见妻子的面
听不见喃婼娜的声音
他急忙向房里走去
像有什么蒙住了心

他在房门前大喊
“我的喃婼娜呀

10. Chasing

When the war ended in triumph for Mengbanjia
The people of Mengbanjia were bustling with excitement
They blew the gold and silver horns
To greet their beloved ones

In the crowd Zhaoshutun
Sought his wife
Ah, Nanruona
Why don't I see you come out and welcome me

Why couldn't he see his wife
Or hear Nanruona's voice
He hurried towards the house
Feeling as if something was kept under wraps① from him

He shouted in front of the door
"My Nanruona

① Feeling as if something was kept under wraps: If a person's heart is wrapped, it means that he is controlled by some witchcraft, and he may do something irrational.

你还不曾起床
还是有了什么疾病

“你是躲在房里绣花
还是忙着梳妆打扮
难道是金花没有戴好
头发还没有梳完”

头人们向他深深告罪
吃吃地把详情说出
最后，又把喃婼娜的话
小心地转告给他

召树屯呆了半天
像一只飞在空中的鸟
遭到猎人的暗箭
突然跌落下来

什么话也说不出
眼泪像小河一样流淌
他拜见父母
像一块石头落在地上

许久许久没有听见声音
阿爹阿妈都着了急
他们把召树屯扶起
故意问他为什么这样伤心

Haven't you got up yet
Or are you not feeling well

"Are you hiding in the room embroidering
Or busy dressing up
Could it be that the golden flower isn't properly worn
Or are you not done with doing your hair?"

The headmen apologized sincerely to him
Stammering to describe the details
Finally, The words of Nanruona
They conveyed to him carefully

Zhaoshutun was dumbfounded for quite a while
Like a bird flying in the air
When hit by a hunter's hidden arrow
It suddenly fell

He could not speak
His tears flowing like a small river
He went to greet his parents
But fell to the ground like a rock

Having not heard a sound from him for a long time
Father and mother were worried
They helped Zhaoshutun to stand up
And asked him why he was so sad even though they knew

“阿爹啊阿妈
我虽然活着回来
我的心已经破碎

“请允许我
去找寻可怜的喃婼娜
她住的地方对别人是太远
对我来说，只在眼前”

阿爹阿妈听见儿子的话
心里像一团乱麻
刚出山的太阳
又被乌云遮住
刚回家的儿子
又要离开爹妈

“我尊贵的英雄呀
听一听你父亲的话
“各勐都有好姑娘
我要出一道布告
把所有的姑娘都召来
任由你挑选”

召树屯立刻回答
“几千几万的姑娘都漂亮
他们统统都是好姑娘
却没有一个活在我心上

"Dad and mum
Although I'm back alive
My heart is broken

"Please allow me
To go find poor Nanruona
To others, the place she lives is too far away
But to me, it's right in front of my eyes"

When father and mother heard his words
Their hearts felt like tangled flax threads
The sun that had just risen
Was about to be covered by dark clouds again
The son who had just returned
Was about to leave father and mother soon

"My honorable hero
Listen to your father
There are nice girls in every district
I will issue a proclamation
To call in all the girls
You can choose whomever you like"

Zhaoshutun said immediately
"Thousands of girls are beautiful
And they are all nice
But none of them lives in my heart

"只要我还有一口气
我就会去找寻喃婼娜"
召树屯带上吃食和弓箭
立刻出门寻找爱人

他又来到金湖边
闻到"洛金坎"①的芳香
怎么能叫他对妻子不怀想
他又坐在湖边低声哭唱

"喃婼娜啊
难道我将死在这里
喃婼娜啊喃婼娜
难道我们再也不能相见"

他又来到佛寺
拜见了叭拉纳西
叭拉纳西对他早已熟悉
他便眯起眼睛

"你是个有福的人
你熟读了许多佛经
我走得十分疲倦
请你让我歇息一夜

① 洛金坎：一种黄色味香的野花，常常寄生于古树上。

"As long as I have a breath
I will search for Nanruona"
Zhaoshutun took some food as well as his bow and arrow
And set out immediately to find his beloved

He came to the golden lake again
Smelling the fragrance of the yellow wild flowers — "luojinkan"
How could he not miss his wife
He sat by the lake once again crying and singing

"Ah, Nanruona
Am I going to die here
Nanruona, Nanruona
Are we not going to see each other again"

He came to the Buddhist temple again
And bowed to Balanaxi
Balanaxi had already been familiar with him
So he closed his eyes

"You are a blessed man
You've read many Buddhist scriptures
I am weary from walking
Please put me up for the night

“你问我为什么来
我是一个过路人
我是失掉鞘的剑
我是找寻妻子的人

“喃婼娜是不是经过这里
我应该怎样去找寻
善良的人啊
请你给我指点”

叭拉纳西站在他面前
说话好像念经
“曾经有朵云彩飘过金湖
曾经有一只孔雀飞过天空

“她有一颗纯洁的心
给你留下一只手镯
她劝你另娶妻子
她劝你把她忘记”

召树屯接过了金手镯
好像托着喃婼娜
心里像火烧一样难过
泪水又不禁流淌

行商的人结伴同行
马铃响得咚咚叮叮

"You asked me why I came
I am a passer-by
I am a sword without a sheath
I am a man looking for my wife

"Has Nanruona passed through here
How should I search for her
Kind man
Please give me some guidance"

Balanaxi stood in front of him
Talking as if chanting
"There once was a cloud drifting across the golden lake
And a peacock flying across the sky

"She has a pure heart
And left a bracelet for you
She urged that you remarry
And that you forget about her"

Zhaoshutun took the gold bracelet
As if holding Nanruona
He felt so sad as if his heart were on fire
That he couldn't hold back his tears

Merchants traveled in company
Their horses' bells ringing

出门的人成双成对
为什么只有他独自一人

“都卑龙啊
你有一颗慈善的心
请你告诉我
我应该怎样去找寻”

叭拉纳西低沉的声音
使召树屯心里难过
他说：“你好好地听着
我要依照喃婼娜的话对你劝告

“那里有滚腾的风砂
那里的山有几万丈高
飞鸟过不去
野兽走不通

“我没有什么法术
也没有什么口诀
我劝你转回头
勐板加还有许多姑娘
勐董板不是你去的地方”

召树屯再三请求
“所有的姑娘头髻都偏朝一边①

---

① 傣族姑娘喜欢把发髻梳朝一边，在傣族成语中有“不合心意”之意。

Others went out in couples
Why was he alone

"Dubeilong
You have a charitable heart
Please tell me
How should I look for her"

Balanaxi's low voice
Made Zhaoshutun so sad
He said, "Listen carefully
I will advise you as Nanruona told me

"Where she went there are rolling sandstorms
Mountains there are tens and thousands of zhang in height
Birds cannot fly over
Beasts cannot get through

"I don't have any magic
Or any formula
I advise you to turn back
There are still many nice young women in Mengbanjia
Mengdongban is not the place for you to go"

Zhaoshutun pleaded repeatedly
"All the young women wear their hair on one side①

---

① All the young women wear their hair on one side: When Dai girls wear their hair on one side, it could suggest that somebody or something is disagreeable to them. (Here it means Zhaoshutun declined Balanaxi's advice and he refused to marry another young woman.)

所有的姑娘和我都没有姻缘
请你把喃婼娜的话说完
我相信：她还给我留下一颗心”

叭拉纳西感到十分为难
他说他是念经的人
他只能祈求帕召①
为人们消灾免难

召树屯辞别了叭拉纳西
他又回到湖边
双手捧起了湖水
神龙的笑声卷起了波浪
它问召树屯又遇到什么困难

召树屯回答
“我的妻子离开了我
我要去把她寻找
她住在勐董板地方
鸟雀也飞不到她的家乡

“神龙啊，树木不能离开土地
月亮哪能离开太阳
我离开了喃婼娜
像葫芦离开了葫芦秧”

---

① 帕召：在傣族文化中，帕召指的是乔达摩·悉达多，即释迦牟尼，万能的佛教创立者。

And none has the conjugal tie with me
Please finish telling me Nanruona's words
I have no doubt: she left her heart for me"

Balanaxi faced a dilemma
He said he was a Buddhist monk
He could only pray to Pazhao①
To help people get rid of calamities

Zhaoshutun bid farewell to the Balanaxi
And returned to the lakeside again
Holding water with both his hands
The magic dragon's laughter rolled up the waves
And it asked Zhaoshutun if he had encountered some difficulty

Zhaoshutun replied
"My wife left me
I'm going to look for her
But she lives in Mengdongban
Her hometown where no bird can reach

"Magic dragon, trees can't leave the land
And the moon can't leave the sun
When I am not with Nanruona
I'm like a gourd cut off from the gourd vines"

---

① Pazhao: In the Dai culture, "Pazhao" refers to Siddhartha Gautama, the founder of Buddhism, who was almighty.

神龙十分同情召树屯
慷慨地给了他两种灵药一支神箭
第一种药能够起死回生
第二种药能够解除疲倦
神箭可以打破一切阻拦

召树屯十分感激
他向神龙拜了三拜
作了九个揖
便又匆匆起程

他走了三百三十三天
不知走过多少森林高山
野兽不来伤害他
妖魔不敢靠近他的身边

晚上他就睡在大树下
猫头鹰飞来和他做伴
他比太阳先起床
他比金鹿先出森林

这一天
他走到一条河边
河水像一条黑布
蜿蜒在森林中间

The magic dragon was very sympathetic to Zhaoshutun
And generously gave him two kinds of panacea and a magic arrow
The first medicine could revive the dead
The second could relieve fatigue
And the magic arrow could go through all obstacles

Zhaoshutun was very grateful
He bowed to the magic dragon three times
And bowed with his hands folded in front nine times
Then he set out right away

He walked for three hundred and thirty-three days
Going across an unknown number of forests and mountains
Beasts didn't hurt him
Demons didn't dare to approach him

In the evening he slept under the big trees
And the owls flew over to accompany him
He got up earlier than the sun
And went out of the forest before the golden stag

One day
He came to a river
The water of which was like a black cloth
Meandering through the middle of the forest

召树屯抽出宝剑
插进水中
剑尖就被熔化
从此，他的宝剑就没有了剑尖

他向四处张望
对着河水叹息
“难道就是这条河啊
拦住我走到妻子面前”

他沿着河边徘徊
一条巨蟒横在河面
他把神龙的药搽在脚底
飞一样踏上蟒身走过河去

召树屯又走了三百三十三天
前面出现了三座奇怪的石山
三座石山互相摩擦撞击
像风车一样旋转

想从天上飞过
可惜没有翅膀
想从地下穿过
地又没有洞穴

Zhaoshutun drew out the sword
Hardly had he dipped it into the water
When the tip of the sword was melted
From then on, his sword lost its tip

He looked around
And sighed at the river
"Is it the river
That will stop me from reuniting with my wife"

As he lingered along the river
He saw a python traversing it
Applying the magic dragon's medicine to the soles of his feet
He leapt as if on wings onto the python and walked across the river

Zhaoshutun walked another three hundred and thirty-three days
There appeared before him three odd stone mountains
They rubbed against each other and collided into each other
Rotating like a windmill

He wanted to fly over the sky
But he had no wings
He tried to get through from underground
But he found no tunnels

路啊，不能被阻拦
他拿起那支神箭
当的射向石山
哗啦一声
石块飞向两边

随着空中的黄尘
召树屯穿过石山
回头一看
石块又合成三座石山

又走了三百三十三天
召树屯来到砂石的海洋旁边
只见一片烟雾
下面的砂石沸腾滚卷

召树屯站在一棵大树下
只听见大风呼呼响
眼睛无法睁开

“喃婼娜啊
难道我就这样被阻拦
我们再也不能见面
难道没有一种方法
让我走到你的身边”

Nothing could stand in his way
He picked up the magic arrow
And shot at the stone mountains
With a loud noise
The stones flew to both sides

With the yellow dust in the sky
Zhaoshutun got through the stone mountains
Looking back
He saw the stones closed back into three mountains

After another three hundred and thirty-three days
Zhaoshutun came close to an ocean with gravels
He could only see a cloud of fog
Under which the gravels were boiling and rolling

Zhaoshutun stood under a big tree
He could only hear the wind whistling
But couldn't open his eyes

"Nanruona
Am I going to be stopped here
And cannot we meet again
Isn't there a way
That will allow me to return to your side"

召树屯坐了下来
猜想着砂石的海洋有多宽
猜想着海洋底下有没有鱼龙
什么东西能够帮助他渡到对岸

他羡慕一阵阵刮过的大风
他羡慕天空中飘过去的白云
“白云呀，请告诉喃婼娜吧
要是我不能过去
就让我死在这里

“我死了也会化为一阵风
要是她的门是朝北边开
我就会吹进她的屋里
要不然我会变为一朵白云
飘到她的屋顶

“早上我看她梳妆
白天我听她歌唱
晚上啊，我会感觉到
她对我的怀想”

天色晚了
鹈托朗开始啼唱
召树屯觉得全身酸痛
他昏昏睡在树下

Zhaoshutun sat down
Wondering how broad the gravel ocean was
Whether there were Ichthyosaurs under the ocean
And what would help to ferry him across the ocean

He was envious of the gusts of wind
And the white clouds drifting in the sky
"White clouds, please tell Nanruona
If I can't get across
Let me die here

"After my death I will become a gust of wind
If her door opens to the north
I will blow into her house
Or I will become a white cloud
Drifting over the roof of her house

"I could see her making up in the morning
And listen to her singing during the day
At night, I could feel that
She is missing me"

It was getting late
And Otoran began to sing
Zhaoshutun felt sore all over
And fell asleep under the tree

半夜里
他被什么声音惊醒
睁眼一看
一对“婼哈里林”①站在树上

雌鸟十分忧愁
她说：“如今生活难讨
明天又到哪里去找寻食物”
雄鸟回答：“你不必担忧
勐董板的喃婼娜回到了家
叭团要杀象为她庆贺”

召树屯暗暗喜欢
他像蚂蚁一样爬到树上
躲在雌鸟翅膀下
用宝剑挖开了毛管
就钻到里边躲藏

不久就听见马鹿鸣叫
大雾降落下来
天色渐渐发亮
两只大鸟扇起了翅膀

---

① “婼哈里林”：傣族传说是一种最大的鸟。

At midnight
He was awakened by some sound
He opened his eyes and found
A pair of "Ruohalilin"① standing on a tree

The female was in distress
Saying, "It's difficult to make a living now
Where could we go to find food tomorrow"
The male replied, "Don't worry
Nanruona of Mengdongban has returned
Batuan will kill elephants to celebrate"

Zhaoshutun rejoiced
He crawled up the tree like an ant
Hiding himself under the wing of the female bird
He cut open the hollow stem of a feather with his sword
Then got into it and hid himself inside

Soon there came the neighing of the red deer
When the curtain of fog fell down
And the light returned gradually
The two giant birds flapped their wings

① Ruohalilin: According to the Dai legends, it is the biggest bird.

飞到海洋中间
雌鸟感到身上发痒
她想抖一抖身子
让什么东西掉进海洋

雄鸟说："初一不杀生
十五不害命
明天是十五
请你把他饶恕"

Flying right above the middle of the ocean
The female bird felt an itch
She wanted to shake her body
To drop the thing into the ocean

The male bird said, "No killing on the first day of a month
No harming on the fifteenth①
Tomorrow is the fifteenth
Please forgive it"

---

① No killing on the first day of a month; no harming on the fifteenth: It is advocated in Buddhism that if we do not kill, we will be blessed, and the benevolent deeds will reward us in the future. Therefore, killing is forbidden on some special days such as the first and the fifteenth days of a month.

十一、到了勐董板地方

乌云里出现了阳光
喃婼娜飞回到她的家乡
阳光铺满地
鲜花朝她开放

父母姐姐都解开心里的疙瘩
一个个都很高兴
公主回来了
正像宝剑插回剑鞘

叭团叫人齐放六门大炮
通知全城的人都为女儿祝贺
百姓都像过节一样
等待着拴线的时刻

叭团又拿一对金手镯给喃婼娜
他不愿意把派兵救她的事告诉她
他说："女儿啊
从此，你再也不要离开勐董板

11. Homecoming

When sunshine emerged from behind the dark clouds
Nanruona flew back to her hometown
The sunshine covered the ground
And all flowers bloomed for her

The knots in her parents' and sisters' hearts undone
Each of them rejoiced
The princess has returned
Just as the sword is returned to the scabbard

Batuan asked his men to launch six cannons simultaneously
Informing people in the whole city to celebrate for his daughter
People felt like it was a holiday
Waiting for the moment of thread tying

Batuan bestowed on Nanruona a pair of gold bracelets
Not wanting to tell her about sending troops to rescue her
He said, "My daughter
You should henceforth not leave Mengdongban again

“愿你常在父母身边
像小鸟一样快活
愿你不要再惹上祸端
好让爹妈多活几年”

父亲把金镯戴在她手上
两手闪闪发光
喃婼娜和以前一样美丽
黑色的眉毛发亮
两只眼睛水汪汪
就像“都拉”①出现在眼前

慈祥的父母坐在她身边
姐姐们都围在她后面
问她捉她的猎人是谁
这些日子她怎么生活

喃婼娜又想起了召树屯
她说猎人是她的丈夫
他们就像鱼和水
他们好像星星和月亮

全家人都十分惊奇
猎人怎么就夺去了她的心
难道她不是兵马抢救回来
难道她只是回来探亲

① “都拉”：“天仙”或“美丽的神”。

"May you always stay with your parents
As joyful as a bird
May you not get into trouble again
So as to let dad and mum live a few years longer"

Her father helped her to put on the gold bracelets
With which her hands were glittering
Nanruona was as beautiful as ever
With shiny black eyebrows
And two watery eyes
She looked like "Dula"① who appeared in Mengdongban

Her kind parents sat by her side
Her sisters were behind her
Asking her about the hunter who captured her
And how she was in those days

Nanruona reminisced the days with Zhaoshutun
She told them that the hunter was her husband
And the two of them were like fish and water
Like the star and the moon

The whole family was astonished
How could the hunter capture her heart
Wasn't she rescued by the troops
Did she come back just for a visit

---

① Dula: heavenly, beautiful fairy.

喃婼娜又埋怨战争
战争拆散了他们
为了战争
召树屯率军出征

叭团吃了一惊
从头发到脚趾他都感到不安
难道那个勇敢善战的少年
就是喃婼娜的男人

要是真的把他杀了
岂不害了喃婼娜的一生
他的嘴唇轻轻颤动
眼光显露着惶惑不宁

召树屯走了九百九十九天
来到了一个城市
这就是勐董板地方
这就是喃婼娜的家乡

召树屯走近城外的“撒拉房”①
只见人们来来往往
女人们穿着五彩的绸缎
身上的珠宝闪闪发光

① “撒拉房”：傣族路边盖的一种供路人休息的房子。

Nanruona then complained about the war
which split them up
Because of the war
Zhaoshutun had to lead the troops and leave her

Batuan was shocked
Feeling uneasy from hair to toe
Could that brave and capable youth
Be Nanruona's husband

If he really was killed
Would it not ruin Nanruona's whole life
His lips quivered
While his eyes betrayed a sign of fear

After a journey of nine hundred and ninety-nine days
Zhaoshutun came to a city
It was Mengdongban
Nanruona's hometown

When approaching the "Sala Room"① outside the city
Zhaoshutun saw people going back and forth
Women were in colorful silk and satin
Their jewelries glittering

---

① "Sala Room": a kind of house in Dai areas that is built beside the road for passers-by to have a rest.

召树屯走了三年
勐董板才过了三天
姑娘们用金锅挑水
准备为喃婼娜拴线

有一个姑娘叫喃新莎
她是喃婼娜的侍女
她挑着金锅走到井边
她是给喃婼娜挑水洗身

召树屯走向喃新莎的身边
他暗暗祈求天神
如果她是给喃婼娜挑水
求天神叫她提不起金锅

果然，喃新莎虽然用尽力气
用尽力气也不能把金锅提起
她抬头看见了召树屯
就请求他帮助一臂之力

召树屯帮她把金锅抬上肩
他悄悄把金手镯放进锅里
他说：“你是个好姑娘
你生得这样美丽”

Zhaoshutun had walked for three years
But only three days had passed in Mengdongban
Girls used gold pots to carry water
Preparing for Nanruona's thread tying ceremony

There was a young woman named Nanxinsha
She was Nanruona's maid
She shouldered the gold pot and went to the well
So as to fetch water for Nanruona to have a bath

Zhaoshutun went up to Nanxinsha
Secretly praying to Heaven
That if she was fetching water for Nanruona
Heaven helped that she was not able to lift the gold pot

As expected, Nanxinsha used all her strength
But could not lift the gold pot
Looking up, she saw Zhaoshutun
And asked him to give her a hand

Zhaoshutun helped her to lift the gold pot onto her shoulder
And quietly slipped the gold bracelet into the pot
He said: "You are a nice young woman
And you are so beautiful"

姑娘满脸通红
心里却像吃了蜂蜜
她说："小伙子呀
你是一只会说话的鹦哥
我是一棵快枯的老树
请你不要拿我取乐

"你是长得这样漂亮
勐董板找不到你这样耀眼的太阳
我没有福气请你挑水
全城的百姓都正在奔忙"

召树屯又问道
"姑娘呀，你来来回回挑了这样多水
是不是像燕子衔泥
为自己筑窠"

喃新莎觉得很惊奇
"全城的人都知道喃婼娜回来
小伙子呀，难道你没有给她祝贺
我挑的水就是为她'洗福'①"

"姑娘啊
原来你挑的是仙水

① "洗福"：傣族的一种风俗，凡远离和久别归来的人，都要在家里用水洗澡，以示吉祥。

Her face flushed
But her heart was filled with joy
She said: "Young man
You are a charming budgerigar
I am a withering old tree
Please do not make fun of me

"You are so handsome
There is not a sun as dazzling as you in Mengdongban
I don't have the fortune to have you carry water for me
Besides, the whole city is busy now"

Zhaoshutun said again,
"Young woman, you carried so much water back and forth
Is it like swallows holding the mud
To make nests for themselves"

Nanxinsha was astonished
"The whole city knows the returning of Nanruona
Young man, haven't you congratulated her
The water I fetch is for her to 'bathe for blessings' ①"

"Ah, young woman
It turns out what you get is holy water

---

① To "bathe for blessings": It is a custom in the Dai culture. When people are leaving or returning home, they will have a bath at home to symbolize auspicious future.

你应该告诉喃婼娜举起手来
再把圣水从她头上冲下
这样她的福气就会更大”

喃新莎回去后依照他的话去做
当水从喃婼娜头上冲下
金手镯便落在她的手上
喃婼娜十分奇怪
为什么这只金手镯又回到她手中

她问喃新莎遇到了谁
来自何方
什么样子
什么姓名

喃新莎回答
“今天挑水不比平常
有一个年轻的小伙子
问我为什么挑水
又教了我这个办法”

喃婼娜又高兴又疑惑
难道丈夫真的来到
他是地上走来
还是天上飞来

You should tell Nanruona to hold her hands out
When you pour the holy water from her head down
She will be blessed with even better fortune"

Nanxinsha got back and followed those words
When water rushed down from Nanruona's head
The gold bracelet fell onto her hand
Nanruona was surprised
Why did the gold bracelet come back to her hand

She asked Nanxinsha whom she had met
Where he came from
How he looked like
And what was his name

Nanxinsha replied
"It was an unusual experience to fetch water today
A young lad asked me
What I was fetching the water for
And taught me to pour the water in this way"

Nanruona was both happy and puzzled
Could it be that her husband had really come
Did he come by land
Or fly from the sky

喃婼娜急忙披上纱毯
向她的父母跑去
一面走一面流泪
一面揩眼泪一面叫喊

“阿爹阿妈啊
我的丈夫……他来了
喃新莎亲眼看见
他现在在井边……”

叭团头人们都很惊奇
他们虽然心里感到怀疑
同时又派了大象来到井边
他们把召树屯接回宫殿

Nanruona hurriedly put on the yarn blanket
And ran to her parents
Tears were streaming down her face as she ran
And she wiped the tears while shouting

"Dad and mum
My husband... he has come
Nanxinsha saw him in person
He is now by the well..."

Batuan and the headmen were all amazed
Although skeptical
They sent an elephant to the well
And brought Zhaoshutun back to the palace

十二、团圆

叭团看见召树屯心里喜欢
年轻美丽一表人才
他摆开酒席
却不让他们夫妻见面

召树屯十分纳闷
两眼四处张望
送酒送菜的人来来往往
就是不见喃婼娜的面

喃婼娜啊
急得像火烧身
窗前望了后门瞧
为什么还不见召树屯进来

叭团举起酒杯
只把闲话问
“年轻的人，你是怎么来的
顺着大风呢
还是驾着白云

12. Reunion

At the sight of Zhaoshutun, Batuan became fond of him
A young man of striking appearance and talent
He laid out a feast
But prevented the couple from meeting

Zhaoshutun was puzzled
He looked around
People were busy serving wine and dishes
But there was no sign of Nanruona

Ah, Nanruona
Was so anxious that she felt she was on fire
She looked through the front window and the back door
Wondering why Zhaoshutun had not come

Batuan raised the glass
And just casually chatted away with Zhaoshutun
"Young man, how did you come
Did you fly with the gales
Or ride the white clouds

“你的父母在哪里
你的家乡是什么情形
为什么独自一人来
你有什么本领”

召树屯回答一句转一下眼
到了勐董板地方
难道是喃婼娜故意不见
难道是丈人对他敷衍

召树屯跪在叭团面前
他请求得到饶恕
冒昧来到勐董板地方
只要求和喃婼娜见一面

叭团有意要看一看女婿的本领
让头人和百姓都来称赞召树屯
他传令用铁挡住道路
再把石头堆成石墙
第三层的石墙又钉上铁钉

他说：“年轻的人
你能够一箭打开这道墙
喃婼娜就是你的妻子
我就把你招为女婿”

"Where are your parents
What is your hometown like
Why do you come alone
What can you do"

Zhaoshutun looked around while answering the questions
Now that he had come to Mengdongban
Could it be that Nanruona was avoiding him
Or the father-in-law was refusing to accept him

Zhaoshutun knelt in front of Batuan
Begging for forgiveness
He came to Mengdongban uninvited
And asked only to see Nanruona once

Batuan wanted to see the capability of his son-in-law
So that both the headmen and people would praise Zhaoshuntun
He ordered the road to be blocked by iron bars
The stones to be piled up into a wall
And the third layer of the wall to be hammered some nails in

He said: "Young man
If you can break the wall with the shooting of one arrow
Nanruona will be your wife
And I'll accept you as my son-in-law"

召树屯只好拿起弓箭
沉着地骑上马
像百鸟中飞来一只凤凰
四面的眼光都看着他

他拉起弓
马往前扑
风往后闪
箭响如雷鸣
三道墙全都崩开

百姓都“水！水！”地欢呼
没有人不称赞召树屯的本领
力气最大的是象
象不能推开石墙

召树屯以为就会见到喃婼娜
没有想到叭团又叫人搭了一个平棚
用布把四面遮住
上面还绣了许多花朵

中间挖了一千个眼睛一样大的小洞

Zhaoshutun had no choice but to pick up his bow and arrow
And calmly mounted on the horse
He felt like a phoenix landing among a bevy of birds
Attracting all the attention around him

He drew the bow
The horse rushed forward
While the wind blew backward
The arrow sounded like a thunderbolt
And all three layers of the wall collapsed at once

People all exclaimed "Water! Water!" ①
No one was not acclaiming the capability of Zhaoshutun
The most powerful creature was the elephant
But even the elephant could not push down the stone wall

Zhaoshutun thought he would see Nanruona immediately
But unexpectedly Batuan asked his men to build a flat shed
And cover all sides with cloth
On which many flowers were embroidered

In the middle there were a thousand holes in the same size of an eye

---

① People all exclaimed "Water! Water! ": There is an indissoluble bond between water and the Dai culture. The Dai people love and admire water, perceiving water as a holy substance, which may bring them happiness, health and good fortune. Here when people all exclaimed "Water! Water!", they intended to acclaim Zhaoshutun for his capability.

他叫了九百九十九个姑娘陪着喃婼娜
每人都从棚里伸出一个手指
然后把召树屯叫到棚下

“年轻的人啊
如果你认不出喃婼娜的手指
就请你快点转回家
以后再也不要想念喃婼娜”

召树屯皱起了眉头
深山里捉鱼
还可以找到沟
一千个手指
像一千株藕芽
叫他选择哪一个

他绕着布棚走了一圈
一千个手指都看了一遍
其中有一个手指
像有一只萤火虫落在上边

这是玉石戒指
啊！不，这是喃婼娜爱情放出的光焰
他紧紧抓住了这个手指
这就是我的喃婼娜

He summoned nine hundred and ninety-nine young women to accompany Nanruona

Everyone extended a finger through a hole from inside the shed

Then he asked Zhaoshutun to come to the shed

"Young man
If you can't recognize Nanruona's finger
Just turn around and go home promptly
Don't ever think about marrying Nanruona again"

Zhaoshutun frowned
When he went to catch fish in deep mountains
He could find the trenches
A thousand fingers were
Like a thousand lotus root buds
Which one should hc choose

He walked around the cloth-covered shed
And looked at the thousand fingers
One of them
Seemed to have a firefly on it

It was a jade ring
Ah, but no! It was Nanruona's love shining through
He held the finger tightly
It was his Nanruona

头人百姓都为他欢呼
叭团和他妻子
扶出了喃婼娜
百姓四面把他们围住

召树屯和喃婼娜
站在百姓的中间
就像千万匹绿叶中间
开放出两朵鲜红的玫瑰

头人和百姓都向他们朝拜
有的人献上好马和大象
有的人为他们祝福
从今后，永远不再分离……

The headmen and people were all cheering for him
Batuan and his wife
Helped Nanruona to come out
And people stood around them in a circle

Zhaoshutun and Nanruona
Stood right in the middle
Just like two red roses
Blooming among thousands of green leaves

The headmen and people showed respect to them
Some offered them strong horses and elephants
Others presented them with sincere blessings
So that they would never separate again...